D0188590

CALGARY PUBLIC LIBRARY

JAN - - 2014

Miranda
the Explorer

Miranda
the Explorer

James Mayhew

Orion
Children's Books

Miranda the Explorer was originally published in 2003
by Orion Children's Books
This edition first published in Great Britain in 2013
by Orion Children's Books
a division of the Orion Publishing Group Ltd
Orion House
5 Upper Saint Martin's Lane
London WC2H 9EA
An Hachette UK Company

1 3 5 7 9 10 8 6 4 2

Text and illustrations © James Mayhew 2003, 2013

The right of James Mayhew to be identified
as author and illustrator of this work has been asserted.

All rights reserved. No part of this publication
may be reproduced, stored in a retrieval system,
or transmitted, in any form or by any means, electronic,
mechanical, photocopying, recording, or otherwise,
without the prior permission of Orion Children's Books.

The Orion Publishing Group's policy is to use papers
that are natural, renewable and recyclable products and made
from wood grown in sustainable forests. The logging and
manufacturing processes are expected to conform to
the environmental regulations of the country of origin.

A catalogue record for this book
is available from the British Library.

ISBN 978 1 4440 0850 0

Printed and bound in China

www.orionbooks.co.uk

For my father.
With love and thanks for all
the acrobatic planes, burning
balloons and flyaway kites!

One day Miranda won first prize
in a painting competition. The
prize was a ride in a balloon
and she was going to be on
television.

Miranda climbed into the
basket under the balloon.

The cameras rolled and she
waved to the cheering crowds.
This was fun!

But then there was a sudden
gust of wind, the rope snapped –
and the balloon sailed away with
Miranda in it, all by herself!
The wind carried her up into
the stormy sky and out of sight.

The balloon flew over cold
rocky islands and hot volcanoes.

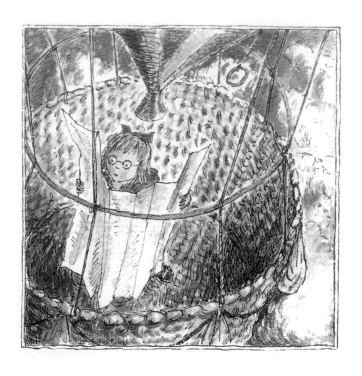

The wind became calmer
and Miranda opened her eyes.
There was nothing in the basket
except a large map of the world.
Miranda wondered where she
could be.

She was very high up but she
decided to be brave. She pulled
a rope under the balloon to see
what would happen.

Hiss! Out came a little gas
and the balloon floated down
through the clouds!

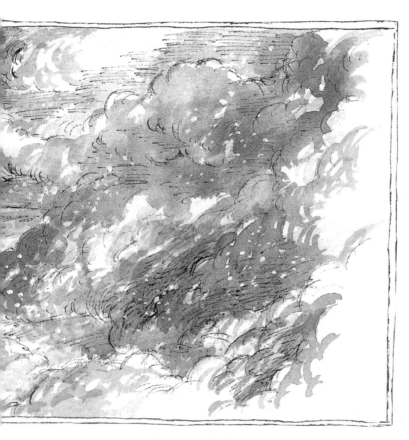

Miranda couldn't stop it and
she landed with a jolt.

A little girl came running
over to her.

"My name's Olga," she said in
English. "Welcome to Russia.
Have you come to visit me?"

"Not really," said Miranda.
"I want to get back home. But
I don't know how to make the
balloon go up again."

Olga noticed the heavy bags
of sand tied to the basket.

"Perhaps if you empty one, the balloon will go up," she said.

As soon as they emptied the bag, the balloon rose up into the air.

"Thank you!" called Miranda. "Goodbye!"

Miranda flew for days and
nights, through wind and snow,
all the way to the Himalayas,
where she brushed the top of the
highest mountain in the world.

Mt Everest, the Himalayas!

Soon the wind felt warmer. Miranda landed in a busy marketplace full of snake charmers and fire eaters, bright colours and spicy smells.

This was India!

On a stall Miranda saw a
compass which showed north,
south, east and west. But she had
no money to buy it.

Then Hari, the boy at the
stall, said, "If you let me ride in
your balloon, you can have the
compass."

"Hop in, then," said Miranda.

He got into the basket and
Miranda took him up into the
evening sky. Then she brought
him gently down again, and
waved goodbye.

The Taj Mahal, near Agra

The Great Wall

Miranda looked at her
compass. She needed to fly west
to get home, but she didn't know
how to turn the balloon around.

of China

She had to go wherever the wind blew her. And the wind blew her over the Great Wall of China, to Japan.

She flew past a village and lots
of children waved from their
windows.

A little girl, Nobuko, had a computer.

"How can I turn the balloon around?" called Miranda from the basket.

Nobuko looked it up on the computer.

"If you go up and down you will find different breezes," she said. "You must find the breeze that will carry you home."

"Oh, thank you!" called Miranda, and she sailed off through the clouds.

Miranda flew up and down
and up again, searching for the
right breeze.

Before she knew it she had
reached Australia.

She swooped down to look at
the koalas and the kangaroos.

AUSTRALIA

The balloon snagged on a
bush, and a thorn ripped a big
hole in it. Miranda sank slowly
towards a river full of crocodiles.

"Are you all right?" called a
boy who was cycling past.

"No, my balloon's torn!"
yelled Miranda.

"No problem, you can borrow
my puncture repair kit," said the
boy. "My name's Bruce. Glad to
meet you."

So Miranda climbed up ropes
and stuck a patch over the hole.
It worked perfectly! She
emptied a sandbag and floated
off.

The wind carried Miranda
across the sea. She flew across
America, and saw Hollywood,
and the Grand Canyon, and
great cities and forests and plains.

The Grand Canyon

45

She didn't stop even when she reached the Statue of Liberty in New York, because she knew she was still a long way from home.

All the tourists took photographs, and the children gave her their doughnuts and icecreams.

The Statue of Liberty

Then Miranda headed across
the sea to Africa.

She let the wind carry the
balloon towards Egypt, because
she wanted to see the pyramids.

She landed in the desert
where a boy called Omar gave
her some water in exchange for
a doughnut.

The Pyramids of Giza, EGYPT

The balloon flew north
to Greece and on to Italy.

The Parthenon, Athens, GREECE

ĀLY

Miranda spotted the Leaning Tower of Pisa. As she landed beside the tower two children asked if they could have a ride. She took them up to the top of the tower and down again.

The Leaning Tower of Pisa

Sofia gave Miranda an
enormous pizza to say thank you,
and Miranda waved goodbye to
Italy.

Miranda flew over the sea
to Spain.

She pulled the rope and came down to have a good look at Barcelona.

She almost got tangled up in
the strings of flags hung across
the streets.

"Don't worry!" she said.

As the balloon flew across France, Miranda noticed it was sinking very low.

She emptied the last of the sandbags, but still the balloon did not rise.

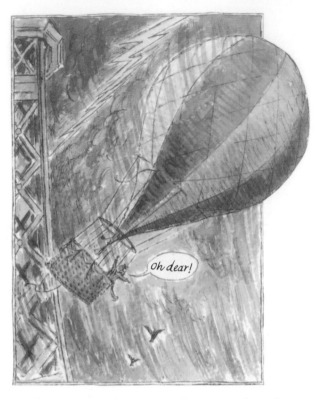

By the time Miranda reached
Paris, the balloon was so low
that it was bumping the rooftops.
She flew straight towards the
Eiffel Tower – and got caught
up in it.

Just to make things worse, it started raining and the wind began to blow. It grew stronger and stronger and …

Whoosh!

Up went the balloon, twirling through the stormy sky, and Miranda was swept across the crashing waves and over high cliffs to England.

65

She flew across London and waved to the Queen as she sailed over Buckingham Palace.

Tower Bridge, London

The balloon limped on, sinking lower and lower until at last it gave a little sigh and flopped on to the ground. Miranda looked around and saw that at long last she was home!

She had her favourite supper and a nice hot bath and fell fast asleep in her own comfy bed.

It was good to be back, but
yet Miranda felt a bit sad. She
missed her adventures.

Next day she rang the
television director and told him
about all the wonderful things
she had seen.

"Do you want your balloon back?" she asked, "I'm afraid it's got a puncture."

"Oh you can keep it," said the director. "And we'd love to make a programme about you. We could call it Miranda the Explorer."

But Miranda said she was too busy. She had a balloon to get ready.

She filled up the sandbags and sewed up the hole, and in no time the balloon was as good as new.

Miranda the Explorer emptied
a sandbag, unfolded her map, and
floated gently up into the sky.
The whole world lay before her.

What are you going to read next?

More adventures with Horrid Henry,

or go exploring with Shumba,

and brave the Jungle

and Arctic with Algy.

Find a frog prince with Tulsa

or even a big, yellow, whiskery

Lion in the Meadow!

Tuck into some

Blood and Guts and Rats' Tail Pizza,

learn to dance with Sophie,

travel back in time with

Cudweed

and sail away in

Noah's Ark.

Enjoy all the Early Readers.

the orion star

Sign up for **the orion star** newsletter
for all the latest children's book news,
plus activity sheets, exclusive competitions,
author interviews, pre-publication extracts
and more.

www.orionbooks.co.uk/newsletters

Follow @the_orionstar on .

Orion
Children's Books